The Lawns of Lobstermen

Poems From the Maine Coast and Belgrade Lakes

Douglas Woody Woodsum
P.O. Box 105
Smithfield, ME 04978
dhw@tds.net

Cover art:
"Lawns of Lobstermen," pen and ink watercolor by JD Asmussen,
copyright © 2010. See artist's website at www.artjourneyer.com
Cover and book design by Nancy Bush,
Violette Graphics & Printing.

ISBN 978-1-4507-0735-0

Published by Moon Pie Press, Westbrook, Maine
Please visit our website at www.moonpiepress.com

Grateful acknowledgement is made to the editors of the following journals and one anthology, in which these poems first appeared, sometimes in different versions, with different titles or both. The four poems followed by "The Fishouse" are posted on the educational website, From the Fishouse, www.fishousepoems.org.

"A Late Raspberry Reminds Him of Her," *The Southern Review*
"Blackberry War," *English Journal* and *The Fishouse*
"Bon Voyage Large Orange Friend," *Kansas Quarterly*
"Bracelet," *The Puckerbrush Review*
"Carving Your Future," *North Dakota Quarterly* and *The Fishouse*
"December: The Queen's Remains," *Goose River Anthology*
"Dusky Variations," *The Higginson Journal*
"First Pig," *Rattle*
"Flickerings," *Down East*
"Forgiveness Prayer #2," *Georgia State University Review*
"Misplaced Landscape With Sandhill Cranes," *Friends of Acadia Journal*
"Nothing Plaintive About Mourning Doves," *Prairie Schooner*
"October Elegy," *Poetpouri*
"Ode: To Trees," *Maine Times* and *The Fishouse*
"Pitcher Plants in January," *Untidy Candles, A Maine Writers and Publishers Alliance Anthology*
"So Innocent a Robbery," *Maine Times*
"Splitting Wood in Winter," *Down East*
"Spooked Moose," *Down East*
"Ten Below, Corea Harbor," *Gray's Sporting Journal*
"The Boats of Corea Harbor," *The Puckerbrush Review*
"The Island Heaven," *Animus*
"The Cove at Angel's Beach," *English Journal*
"The Lawns of Lobstermen," *Down East*
"The Old Squaws of Corea Harbor," *The South Florida Poetry Review*
"The Skaters of Corea Harbor," *Friends of Acadia Journal* and *The Fishouse*
"Whirlwind," *English Journal*

I would also like to thank hundreds of people and dozens of institutions for help, inspiration and encouragement over the last twenty years. The list is too numerous, but the short list includes my parents, Joan and Ed Woodsum, and my sisters: Lee, Rae, and Alix. Thanks go as well to the English Departments of Middlebury College, The Bread Loaf School of English, The Bread Loaf Writers' Conference, Denver University, University of Michigan, The Sewanee Writers' Conference, Colby College, and Messalonskee High School. Special thanks to my biggest supporter, Donna Asmussen.

Contents

Down East

The Lawns of Lobstermen

Because they cannot live without the sea
they bring it home with them. It starts with boats:
skiffs, punts or dinghies . . . the outboard workboat, all
flat-bottomed or leaning, keeled to one side . . .
always little boats in the green harbors
of their lawns. And stacks of lobster traps: three, four, five
high, with buoys and potwarp stored inside.
Weeds grow around the traps: wildflowers less pungent
than the clinging seaweeds, dry and brittle now, pulled
from the deep. More buoys lie scattered
about, beyond repair or fresh-painted
eyed by tourists on their way to the old inn
with the pintsized lighthouse on its lawn.
Gulls land in these backyard backwaters, pecking
at scraps of bait and clumps of mussels
slow-roasted by sun. Mooring anchors sit,
old and new, hauled for good or ready to set:
a fifty-five gallon drum full of cement,
an old V-8 engine, a block of granite.
A rust-red chain, roughly coiled and snaking
away, sinks into uncut grass and shadows
awaiting the young son and his mower.
His father says, "I hit that cussed thing, too."
Call them what you want, those fishermen's lawns:
shrines, workshops, junkyards . . . eyesores or delights.
Children play while mothers in flannel sip coffee
in the sun. An old oar, its mate missing,
leans against the stoop, rowing the house to sea.

The Skaters Of Corea Harbor

The harbor seldom freezes. When it does
    Only the hollow-boned gulls on their webbed
        Feet can enjoy the thin, brittle ice. Men

In heavy boots and layers of wool break
    Through if they are so foolish as to try.
        Instead they wait for calm November dawns

Like today, when the boats float on the sky.
    They wait and then they skate in wooden skiffs
        From their wharves to their fishing boats, stroking

Across the icy calm with long wooden
    Oars, the smooth sanded edges, sanded by
        The sea, cutting clean glassy tracks that swirl

As if a skater had stopped to twirl. Once
    I saw a man with one leg skate by,
        Or, I should say, he stood in his skiff

Propelling it with a single oar.
    As graceful as any skater born and raised
        In the North, he glided by strokes to where

His boat was moored. They do not know I watch
    Them skate with their oars and their flat-bottomed
        Skiffs, leaving whirlpools in ice; just as I

Did not know when I first ventured on ice
    That it's not ice we skate on when we skate
        On ice. It's water that comes from the blade

Pressing down, melting a thin track
    So we float as we stroke.
        Thawing the ice, we sail.

The Boats Of Corea Harbor

On stormy days, the fishermen drive their trucks
Onto the boat launch at Kettle Cove.
They roll down windows, sip from Styrofoam cups,
And talk while the fishing fleet weathers and rolls.

Some fishermen drive out onto the docks:
Joking, smoking, tossing cigarette butts.
When the squalls pass through, they roll their windows up,
Then watch the boats through the wipers' slow arcs.

There's a chore or two to keep them busy
For an hour or two at the wharf or the shop.
And they'll linger longer at the counter at Rudy's,
But by the water is where they end up,

By Joy Frances, Rebecca B., Lisa Lynn,
Paula Laverne, KarenJo, and Cindy Lee;
By Cathy Ellen, Maria S., Debra Ann,
Bernice Ellen, Laverna Gail, and Nana Marie.

The Old Squaws Of Corea Harbor

Voice: Talkative; musical cries, "onk-a-lik,
ow owdle-ow," etc.

Roger Tory Peterson

They show up each year when it's cold
And the hunting season's over,
Little ducks repeating the old
Stories of their species, chatter

Unlike the noise of other ducks.
They learned their tones from the Chinese,
Endurance from the auction block.
Even the young ones speak with ease

When they are allowed to talk. Gulls
Try to steal their food; sometimes do.
But conversation never lulls
For more than a second or two

Even after losing a crab
To the bully gull. Their banter
Seems smooth; they take turns, never snub
One another. Their flock leader,

If there is one, must supervise
With a quiet feather. They sing
Their conversations amid noise
Of the harbor, and listening

May surprise you when you find out
Their retold tales improve with time,
They never whisper, never shout,
And, without fail, they speak in rhyme.

Splitting Wood In Winter

You'll need a barn with a big door, the old
fashioned kind that hangs on wheels, slides open
down a track. You'll need a bare bulb, the sun
having sunk before your return from work.
You'll need a splitting maul (the ax always
gets stuck), a medieval weapon perfect
for pillaging heat from the heart of hardwood.
You can plug in the portable radio
or just listen to the hush of the swing
then thwack . . . or thoonk, and the soft clinks or cloonks
of the splits falling from the chopping block
onto the old, thick, scarred floorboards of the barn.
You'll need your hands to rip apart pieces
still connected by strips of unsplit wood.
You'll need to load the canvas carrier
thrice, enough to survive the dead of night.
You won't need reminding, "Cutting wood warms
you twice: once cutting it, once burning it."
You'll smile walking through the cold, back to the house,
your hot breath a harbinger of wood smoke.

Bracelet

Beyond the woodstove and its heat rising
To give the room a dreamlike air, beyond
The wooden barrel that came with the barn
That came with the house, the wooden barrel
We use for wood. Beyond the wicker chair
That also came with the house and that looks
Pretty good, worn as it is on the arms.
Beyond the doorway to the dining room,
A doorway without a door, although holes
In the wood and the shadows of hinges
Indicate this was not always the case.
Beyond the round, hardwood table with dried
Flowers tied in a bow at its center.
Beyond the windows half covered with frost,
Frost that gathers in the night then slowly
Thaws back into the air during daylight.
Beyond those half-obscured windows, the wind
Blows the stunted shrubs and weeds in wavy
Motion made more wavy by the wood stove's
Invisible, smoke-like heat. And against
The undergrowth there, beyond the iced drive,
I see the wreath that blows off the rusted
Nail by the door every two or three days.

On my way back from the barn with the next
Load of wood, I'll wear that wreath on my
Arm like a giant bracelet, then rehang
It on the nail, brushing snow from the frayed red
Ribbon, knocking the pine cones caked with ice.

Remembering Luck

Clown: A tanner will last you nine year . . . his hide is so tann'd with his
trade that [he] will keep out water a great while, and your water is a sore
decayer of your whoreson dead body. –Hamlet, V.i.68-72

I am oiling my boots today. It has been
a couple years at least since I last oiled
them, and I have been lucky: no leaks, no
major cracks, no tears. I have oiled them most
every year, and they have lasted over
twenty years. I use my hands –my fingers—
to work the oil in. It looks like yellowed
bacon fat too long in the pan. It smells
clean and oily both.
                              I think of the Clown's
tanner in Hamlet every time I oil
my boots. I think the Clown's right; if I oiled
boots for a living my hands would last nine
years in the grave. I smile both at the Clown
and at the pleasure of rewarding work,
simple work.
                    I dream of being a clown
as Shakespeare defines one, a simple man
with a spade digging graves for a living . . .
or a baker, or a mower of lawns.

I wiped my boots with a cloth to clean them,
but my hands are the tools that work the oil
into the leather, the dead cowhide nine
years dead, plus nine more years, plus two, plus more.

I have neglected many other simple
tasks; don't get me wrong. There are little things
I let slip, and suddenly something breaks.
I have suffered the car, the house, the wrath
of a wronged lover. I have failed to oil
what needed to be oiled. But today . . . no.
Today I am oiling my boots.
                                        The snow
fell during the night and today it rained.

My boots were fine as I walked in the slush,
but I remembered that I was lucky
today. I remembered it had been two
years, at least, and I should not expect more.

The water beaded up and fell away
after I stepped in a puddle. There was no need
 to let the boots dry. I merely wiped them
clean with the cloth. Now I feel the bit of grit
the rag left behind under my fingers
working the oil into the smooth leather,
into the stitches of the seams, into
the cracks that are like cracks in my own skin.
I am old; my skin is cracked, but it's whole.

I like to set the boots by the open-faced
wood burning stove when I am done. They'll dry
anywhere, and they're not really drying,
but I like the light on the oiled leather.

I am oiling my boots by the woodstove
today, and the heat and the smell of oil
makes all seem beyond decay. I am lucky.
It has been two years since I last oiled my boots,
two years at least. My fingers slide over
the dead skin coming alive again, cracked
and a little bit gritty and shining.
Even when I am done, I pick them up again.

Ten Below, Corea Harbor

For introducing me to the cold
I love my father. With guns aboard
We'd row to the anchored boat to fire
It up and head to the ledges for duck.

So cold, only fools--hunters and fishers--
About, that one and only time
The harbor froze: windowpane-thin ice
That cracked and tinkled against the hull.

The water and ice both made soft sounds.
Sometimes the ice seemed to rip, but still
It chimed. The thwack of oar against
Gunwale. The sun a mere hint of pink.

Working the engine's choke, setting
Tollers, minding the ropes, I'd strip
Off my mittens, briefly. That was too much;
The cold would throb my fingertips.

The seawater froze in a glaze that cracked
Underfoot on seaweed-covered ledge,
So we left powdery tracks until
The tide came back. We hunched amid rocks.

Watching, waiting for ducks, we'd fend
Off cold with small talk, eyes squinting
Into low sun, gun safeties clicked on.
We were part of the winter dawn.

It was then I learned to laugh at cold,
Laugh as my father laughed. We never
Considered turning back, those days
When even he was young, my father.

I wish you could know what I knew then:
The closeness in the quiet two men share,
The good shots, the teamwork of crew on land
And sea, the care we took in the cold.

10

Dusky Variations

The bird knew to land
On the highest brink

Of the tree and sing
To keep the darkness

Away. I stopped to hear out
Its song, but I could not.

Even to outlast the setting
Sun, it sang a garbled tune:

In subtle dusky variations
Into the swift night it sang.

South of Portland

The Cove at Angel's Beach

He has a destination in mind.
Rowing with the two oars in unison,
he looks down across his salty trail, the waves
he's made subsiding back into calm, the line
where he parted the world, not a straight one
and dissolving fast. He looks up at the land.

On the beach, his daughter notices
the brief interval when her father's strokes
coincide with the rhythm of the small waves
folding on the shore. She pauses, a sandy
forearm raised to brush away her blowzy
hair, looks beyond the glare of sun on water
to her father.

            He's going to be captain
today. He'll tie the dinghy to the moored
boat, feel the hardwood deck sway
in the expected way. He'll stand surveying
the sea, surveying the land; the damp wheel
in his hand, and then he'll take in the view
of his full-grown daughter, up to her calves
in the sea, up to her beautiful calves.

They're going to fish for mackerel off
the island where they've fished together for years,
where he snapped a picture of her in her
orange life preserver the day after the tooth
fairy came. They'll fish and catch a bucket
full and listen to the Red Sox on the radio.
But he hasn't reached the boat yet.

                He rows
out across the cove while she collects blue
sea glass in the shallows. He watches her
as he rows away, and, on occasion
she looks up, listening to the soft sound
of his oars. When he reaches the boat, she waves
as if he's going away without her.

Bon Voyage, Large Orange Friend

A whale has died and turned orange. It heaves
And rolls in medium sized waves and looks
Like a giant sweet potato. It drifts
Just off the beach, and I'm sure it will wash
In and rot in front of the house for months.
My wife calls the Coast Guard in South Portland.
Hours later they arrive in a forty
Foot speed boat. The whale has hardly moved.
It still floats, but a point of rock ledge keeps it
From drifting farther up the coast. Three men
In an inflatable boat come ashore
Feeding a thick line over the transom
Of their small vessel. The line goes back
To the bigger boat. On the beach, we tell them
We are worried about the stink, and they
Seem to understand; they already have a plan
As if this type of marine accident
Happens all the time. They tell us they will
Tow the whale to sea and sink it.
We watch them for awhile and learn how hard
It is to tie a towline on a whale
Whose tail has rotted off or been gnawed off.
They had hoped to loop their thick line around
The skinniest part of the whale between
The tail and the tapering body, but
Now they must improvise. One of the men
Maintains radio contact with the boat
Offshore, even though at times they just yell
Back and forth over the water. It's calm
And hot. The whale shines in the shallows.
When the men start cursing, my wife and I leave.
We go up to the house and open beers
And sit on the porch where we can see most
Of the action. We hear human voices
And hear the loud staticky radio
Voices and begin to wonder how we
Would handle this whale if left on our own.

14

We come up with no better plans than to
Cover it with rocks or to chop it down
To chunks and boil the chunks down to lamp oil
In the big blue pot we cook lobsters in.
A man yells from the big boat to the three
On shore, "Tie a couple of goddamn
Half hitches around it," and we begin
To tell our favorite Coast Guard tales. Once
A marooned boater drifted near the surf
After his engine failed. A crowd gathered
On the shore to watch, so, when the Coast Guard came,
A man with a megaphone ordered us
All back. Twice he said to stand back because
They were going to shoot a line, a blank
Harpoon to the man adrift. We moved back twice,
And when the Coast Guard fired, the line shot high
Over our heads: past the man and his boat,
Past the water, behind us, landing
On dry land. The locals say the Coast Guard mans
Its boats with fresh recruits from Nebraska
And Kansas, young men who dream of the sea
As I might dream of an ocean of wheat.
Once the Coast Guard couldn't find our harbor,
And by the time they arrived, an hour too late
The three people in the sinking boat
Were safe ashore, thanks to a fisherman.
We have many stories, but the big boat
Is revving up, so we watch it take up
The slack in the rope. We are preparing
To wish our large orange friend bon voyage,
When the rope slips off the whale and curses
Issue from the beach. The inflatable
Boat returns to the mother ship and new
Tacticians ride back to the whale with new
Tools. One man holds a hand auger, a drill
One might use to drill a hole for a lock
In a door, a bit brace with a knob on top
And a second handle for turning
The large auger as fast as you can.

He drives the awkward drill with his fast hand
To cut into the side of the whale. We guess
What will happen next: Will they put something
In the hole to attach a line? Will they
Fill the whale with explosives and blow it
Up? We never find out. It takes a long
Time to auger a whale. The sun sets.
Lights from the offshore boat light the work scene
And blind us, hiding almost everything.
During dinner —lobsters we had boiled red
In the blue pot— we hear them working: clank
Of metal, splashing of feet, the muffled
Voices of a distant operation.
Dusk fades completely. Finally, about
Nine o'clock, the Coast Guard boat motors off
Into the dark silence. Through my glasses
I can see figures on the deck. Two stand
In the stern watching the thick line towing
Something in the dark behind them. The whale
Is out there, but I can't see it. Perhaps
Under the dark sea or on the surface,
Churning in the wake of the boat —the wake
Of the whale— a path of fleshy crumbs leads
Small fish to the burial grounds. At dawn
The gulls will cry for the lost whale, the grains
Of carrion that sunk to the crabs, cry
In fit song for the coarse work done along
The coast. It's a hungry cry, a human
Cry, closer to laughter than sadness.
I hold my hot breath in for a moment
When the lights of the boat sail out of sight.

Nothing Plaintive About Mourning Doves

Two mourning doves have landed in the packed
mud of the drive and approach the puddle
where the scotch pine boughs are mirrored. The doves
bend and drink then straighten and look around
because the neighbors own a murderous
cat. Their breasts, tinted with pink and not a plume
out of place, are seamless and curvaceous.
Their little red feet leave tracks I shall look
at later. But for now, I stop stirring
my tea and lift the spoon from the teacup,
and that is all they need for an excuse
to fly away: unfolding their wings which
slap together when they flap them, their fan
tails unfolding, the morning unfolding.

A Late Raspberry Reminds Him of Her

Fairest fruit by far
that I, this summer, saw . . .

Too red to not be picked
among dark thorns and greens

Too ripe to not be pressed
between the tongue and the mouth's roof . . .

Into that warm cave come
and share your taste with me.

So Innocent A Robbery

When I was young I watched the surfcasters
Evenly spaced down the beach at dusk,
Casting their lines beyond the breaking waves,
Fishing for striped bass on Higgins Beach.
I never saw one catch a single fish.
Theirs was a quiet, ritualistic sport:
Baiting their hooks, setting their rods in stands,
Tinkering with tackle and their reels. It was calming
To watch their patience, watch the resolve to fish
Where there appeared to be no fish. I admired
The long, thin poles half obscured where dark beach
Formed the backdrop, but clearly outlined
Where they bent seaward against the sunset.
The surfcasters seemed harmless to me
Like young, Italian men by the Trevi
Fountain in Rome who whistled at my sister,
Young men who were fishermen of sorts themselves.
They cast matchbox-sized grapplers on lines
Into the pools below the fountains,
Then hauled them in along with the coins
And the wishes of the tourists who watched
Charmed by so innocent a robbery.
The surfcasters seemed innocent all those weeks
I watched them. Theirs was the neutrality
Of kite flyers, landscape painters or old men
Content on docks dreaming of their youths
Spent buoyed by the fathomless sea. For weeks
I watched the surfcasters when I was young:
My first summer in Maine, five years old,
Earning a few nickels and dimes by combing
The beaches at dusk for returnable bottles,
Combing the deserted beaches where the swimmers
Had left their tracks and other imprints
In the sand; the lifeguards long gone, only
The surfcasters, quiet yet guardian-like
With their scepters leaning toward Neptune.
They smoked their cigarettes and watched the gulls
Fly home for the night. There was no death

On the beach that summer, a time so easily
Romanticized by so little a thing
As the man in the bakery truck
Who delivered English muffins to our door.

Twenty-five years later, I returned
To Higgins Beach for a sunset.
The surfcasters were still there, catching
Nothing it seemed until I saw one tugging
On his sharply bent pole, and then he caught
One, a good sized striped bass. He unhooked it
And it flopped on the beach, truly like a fish
Out of water. I was raised to finish
The work I start, so I've wrung the necks
Of wounded sea ducks; I've hit the fish hard
With a boat hook to make a quick, clean kill.
This fisherman knew none of that. He let
The fish do its death dance, puffing its gills
Out, flopping every which way, even up
To a perfect nose stand once: a moment
When its tail was straight up as if a trick.
The slick sand of Higgins Beach reflected
The bass standing on its nose, reflected
The fiery sunset sky. I told the man
He ought to slit its throat or club it. He played
He didn't hear me. Sucking on a glowing
Cigarette, he cast out into the surf
Again, ignoring the fish, ignoring me.
So I moved down the beach where the other
Surfcasters were catching nothing, where one
Ritual led to another and the first
Stars seemed hesitant to shine in the blue-black sky.
I had a knife. I could have done the work
Myself, but when I decided to act
I turned and walked quietly back behind
The fisherman, then I grabbed the dying
Fish where the body tapered to the tail,
And ran to the surf and threw it in. I ran
From the sputtering, angry man, ran until
His curses washed thin with the sound of the sea.

Ode to Trees

You giants, you dwarves; you leaners, you poles;
you gnarled fists, you saplings with two leaves;
you bare harbingers of cold, you budding
heralds of green . . . I sing your praise.

You earth holders, you soil
protectors; you bird sanctuaries,
you shelters for the deer; you child dandlers
(I've seen you bounce them up and down); you kite
snaggers, you window scratchers and nightmare
screechers making children cry . . . I sing
your praise.
        You tightropes for snow, you drinkers
of rain; you gossipers in wind, you blurs
in the fog; you dancers always stretching,
always limbering up but not dancing;
you watchers, you waiters, you accommodators
(I've seen you bend over backwards):
you power line breakers forcing us to pleasure:
candles, oil lamps and rare silences
in the muffling dark . . . I sing your praise.

You crow perches, you squirrel parapets;
you needle and leaf shedders;
you stream-cloggers, you ground-matters, you liners
of nests; you woodpecker feeders, you air
purifiers, you sap yielders; you nut
and pine cone droppers, you bark bearers;
you thicket makers, you shade givers . . . I sing
your praise.
        You white oaks, you paper birches,
you sugar maples; you aspen, you beech;
you Scotch pine, blue spruce, and balsam fir;
you walnut, sweet crab apple, and black cherry;
you lilac, you flowering dogwood,
you horse chestnut; you ash, you locust, you elm;
you weeping willow . . . you trees . . . I sing your praise.

Forgiveness Prayer

Forgive me, dear Lord, for taking your squirrel today.
He kept jumping around in the crown of the Scotch pine,
so it took me a dozen shots with the pellet gun.
Your varmints are feisty, God, even as they wet
themselves worrying. Pine grows thick and darker up high.
The squirrel froze, invisible in the tight top branches.
I sat on the car hood, waiting to spy movement.

If your wild things stayed in the bushes, I would not level and aim.
It is a bad feeling. The problem is red squirrels
clawing through the house walls and floors, keeping sleep at bay.
They seem so light of step until the midnight hours.
I dislike killing, but I have taken many,
making it quick, finishing off the wounded. I aimed
for the final shot, but it stopped convulsing and died.

Pitcher Plants in January

Betrayed by a thirst, the pitcher
Plants stand as if alive, frozen erect.
Subtle meat-eaters, they wait

Killers and trappers, hunters that are urns,
Thin-skinned with red veins even in winter,
Dead now. Diluted nectar and enzymes

Freeze, a crystal web of water.
A pool of rain holds
The petal-rimmed shapes hard as shell,

Ice keeping things whole.
It is too cold for insects now. Only
A chickadee pecks the ice inside

A flowering stomach. Between the woods
And frozen pond, preserved pitcher plants
Rise above brittle grasses and leaves,

Swaying in breezes on thin stems.
They must thaw and live again. Death has been
Too kind to them; there must be another.

Flickerings

Splintered wood and soft-packed snow
Lie underneath the lantern's glow.
I've made this trip a hundred times
To stoke the stove when the fire gets low.

I've swung my ax a thousand times
Split hardwood oak and softwood pine.
I like the heat the hardwood throws
And white pitch bubbles as the softwood whines.

My trip is short; the load's not light.
My breath clouds up the clear, starred night.
My heart knocks hard, but my arms are strong.
A few flakes fall from calm, black heights.

No clouds above, the snow seems wrong,
But I don't think about this long.
There's more than wood to fetch tonight.
I poke the coals, put the kettle on.

Whirlwind

Old snow
with some life
left to it
rearranges itself
outside: circling
like a thin
white dog.
Finding a spot
out of the wind,
it settles.

Here by the hearth
where my dog curled
for so many years,
his apparition appears
then melts.

The Island Heaven

I cannot row to the island;
The island is too far.
When I was younger I rowed there.
It was no great labor.

Now I cannot carry the boat
From the house to the beach.
I could drag it over the bluff,
But the hull would be scratched.

I used to carry my compass,
A fish line and my knife.
I called the island heaven,
And left my landlocked life.

Now I sit and do my rowing
In this old rocking chair.
I dream the island is closer,
And I've found safe passage there.

Not Far From Smithfield

Misplaced Landscape With Sandhill Cranes

Out of place, like a cyclist on a winter road
at dusk, two cranes bend then straighten their bony legs
stepping over rows of thick brown stalks, frosted stubble:
a chopped corn field touched with snow. Beside them, a flooded
ditch, iced-over; so they eat gleaned corn, a deer mouse,
and a lost half-frozen woolly bear.

The farmlands stretch for miles, but the cattle have been called in.
Only the cranes, dusky in this light, graze. I'm used to Currier
And Ives landscapes with stocky turkeys emerging
from the woods to scratch and peck a living under
the old apple trees. In these parts, meandering turkey flocks
sometimes hold up traffic on the rural highways.

But these cranes are far from the road, easy
to miss, despite being tall as the surrounding fence posts.
Svelte and large-framed, they're graceful for all their angles and bones.
Yes, graceful, because when I stop pedaling to be part
of the spare brushstrokes of this oriental winter scene,
the cranes take off, taking the whole world away with them.

With ease, their legs bend then straighten; their wings gesture across
the landscape of fields, darkening woods and outbuildings. They take off
as the sun takes light at dusk, as a brush runs out of paint.

First Pig

You ever tried to get a pig in a truck?
I did last winter in the snow and frozen mud.
I made a ramp from scrap-wood
and leaned it against the back of the Chevy.
I remembered someone telling me,
"It takes two very strong but not very smart
men to get a pig in a truck."
So I called my buddy, Lenny Dragon.
We scrummed around with that pig
for about a half-hour before we quit.
Lenny said, "I got my rifle in my truck;
a dead pig's an easy-to-move pig,
and the damn thing's going straight to the slaughterhouse."
That sounded good to me; I was ready
to go at it with a baseball bat myself.
But that was my first pig; I wanted to do it right.
Everyone I knew delivered their pigs live.

When I got my pig, all I wanted was pork.
Seven months later, when I called Lennie
for help getting the pig to slaughter,
all I was thinking about was ham steak,
chops, and sausage; jury-rig a ramp,
apply a little muscle to the pig,
and away we go. I didn't know how
hard it is to get a pig in a truck.
Pigs are so low to the ground, they don't budge.
Till they start fightin' and put it in four wheel drive.

In a small town, word gets around.
Long after I got that pig in the truck,
I couldn't go anywhere without a barb
or two of pig lore. The next time I make a fool
of myself, I pray to God it won't be in winter.
Farmers got too much free time then,
too much sitting in greasy spoons
or around woodstoves talking about whose ass
is muddy and whose boot's full of snow.

Since that day with the pig, I've heard it all,
why it's so hard to get a pig in a truck:
"Pigs don't like change," or "Pigs can smell death."
One friend pointed to this almanac passage:
"When preparing to slaughter your pig,
keep in mind that pigs seem to know
what is about to happen to them."
If I'd've known, I might've raised chickens.

What finally happened was Lenny was cold,
wet, and threatening to leave. I said, "Hold on;
I got an idea." I called the oldest farmer I knew.
He was decent, allowed as how he'd had a few pig scrapes
in his day. He said, "Put a five gallon bucket
on that pig's head. Lift up one rear leg,
and use it like a tiller. Steer that pig backwards
with that raised leg. Drag and push the bast'd
right up your ramp. Don't stop once you start."

The old man was right. Once we got the bucket
on the pig's head and one rear leg in the air,
it was easy as pissin' in a boot.
That farmer got a slab of bacon
for his advice. Yup, he made it easy
but for one part: You ever tried
to put a five gallon bucket on a pig's head?

December: The Queen's Remains

The ribs of the Queen Anne's lace
Curl up when the lace is gone:
Burnt by a fiery season,
Faded from green to brown . . .

From brown to gray or gold
Depending on light and the field:
Dun cups or goblets rare,
Skeletal toasts to December . . .

December, the giver of lace:
Goose feather stars in a cup;
How slow they drift down and fill up
The rib cage that's taken the place

Of the whitest and beauty marked face:
A mole in a sea of snow,
A kiss on her cheek as she goes,
She who returns when it snows.

Note: "Goose feather" is a phrase used to describe snow that falls in clumps of flakes that are as big as and that resemble feathers.

Inland Scuttle

He didn't park the tractor; it just died
in the field across the road from his farm.
We assumed he'd tow it, as always, to the barn;
we were dead wrong. It sat exposed
through to autumn's end, a blue tarp over
its engine . . . sat through late rain, leaves unraked.
In winter, it wore a clean, white cover
like the plastic mother puts over cake.
Then melt, mud, May and June. The tractor seemed
to spring a leak as timothy and vetch,
milkweed and yarrow became a sea, teemed
above the small front tires, the brake, the clutch.
July, all we could see: the two caution
lights on the rear fenders, the green ocean.

Grease Gun Thanksgiving

Thank you, dear Lord, for the calm that helped me grease the tractor.
I'm not "handy" to quote the locals; I teach school. I did
not even want the tractor, but this farm came with too much
land for a middle-aged man to mow. I ignored the thick
owner's manual for months: the battery froze solid
last winter. I had bought a three year tractor service plan,
but it didn't cover basic lubrication. I've not
seen a clean man use a grease gun, God, and I am a bit
of a neat freak. Grease guns are always covered with grease, too.
It was a trial requiring wheel ramps to drive up onto.
It took three trips to the hardware store, thirteen miles away.
Loading a grease gun is not easy and shouldn't be done
on a kitchen table. After my hissy fit, I calmed
down, Lord God; I put the coupling on the nipples and pumped.

A Country Awakening

When I viewed the house, a note on the kitchen table said,
"Blackberries," and the realtor echoed "blackberries," sweeping
her hand like a magician's assistant, as if two bowls
of plump, ripe blackberries had just appeared next to the note.
I bought the house because it was the only one I could afford,
and, yes, there was a good-sized patch of blackberries.
That first summer there, the war began. Saying "blackberries"
is akin to saying "coconuts," not coconuts bought
from a store, but the real thing: milk and white meat sealed inside
a skull of brown wood. Add to that a fibrous husk an inch
or two thick, impenetrable as a war shield. What's worse,
coconuts grow on top of tall, limbless palms. Try climbing one.
In short, saying "blackberries" or "coconuts" is like saying,
"There's a safe filled with riches in the Titanic's
waterlogged hull; help yourself." To say blackberries have thorns
is like saying porcupines have quills. Imagine doing
battle with giant, angry porcupines (the blackberries
grow eight and nine feet tall) and you will start imagining
paying four bucks for a pint of blackberries at the store.
You will imagine pick-your-own strawberry fields with beds
of hay spread between the rows to keep the weeds down. You will
imagine lolling there, eyes closed, in the sun, half asleep,
dreaming of rototilling your blackberry patch, planting grass
instead. Someone or something angry and vengeful
must have been turned into a blackberry patch in a lesser-known
Greek myth. Usually, before I have picked half a cup,
the blackberries have got me. The sweatshirt, my crude armor,
with long sleeves and a hood, has been ensnared, ripped, and torn
from my body. Like being in a school of piranha,
I pull back from the bloodthirsty thorns in front, and there are more
behind. "Bucolic" the realtor had said, which means "happy
life in the country." I had thought she meant my house. But she
would have said "Bubonic" if she was describing the plague,
the black death of blackberry picking. She also said, "Sold."

The Mower's Revenge

"It's been a week," the lawn says;
"Get off your butt and start to mow."
You do not like the lawn's tone
So you keep sitting and say "no."

"You'll have to rake," the lawn warns;
"The clippings will pile up, turn brown."
You think, "The lawn has a point."
You shift in your rocker and frown.

"Rain's a-comin'," the lawn scolds.
"A-comin'," you think, "Who says that?"
You see clouds, so you stand up
And change into work clothes and hat.

"Who's your daddy?" the lawn boasts;
"Who da boss? Who da man?" You drown
The voice by mowing, but first . . .
You raise the wheels, drop the blade down,
Then cut the grass flush with the ground.

Forgiveness Prayer #2

Forgive me, Dear Lord, for killing your colony of bees
today. They'd lived in a hole in the middle of my yard
ten feet from the front door. Farther off would have been safe, but
anyone mowing, barbecuing, playing, or strolling
would have been at risk. I don't like to kill, God, and the news
has reported several times that bees are declining.

It was easy to decide to protect my family
and friends, but, once again, a haze of second thoughts makes me
wonder if good Christians put up with the occasional
bee sting. If doubts were mental pushups, Father, I would have
the strongest brain in the land. Those bees were testy and not
easily subdued by the spray. I bought a second can
and finished them at chill dawn while they dozed or were logy.
I did what the can said, and now I pray for forgiveness.

Spooked Moose

Like a real bull in a bullfight, the full-grown bull moose
Lowered his head and ripped through my neighbor's laundry, pinned
To the line from the house corner to the apple tree.

And like a bride with a twenty-foot train, it dragged the line
And the clothes across my neighbor's lawn, leaving a wake
Of clothespins, jeans, tee shirts, and boxer shorts every few yards.

Then, like a moose in a panic because it has rope
And clothing tangled in its horns and more rope and clothes flapping
About its torso and rear legs, very like such a moose,

It lowered its head again and charged through the old barbed wire
Pasture fence, snapping the rotten fenceposts off at ground level,
Dragging and, finally, snapping, the rusty wires of a forgotten farm.

And then like a fearful beast learning fear for the first time,
It picked up speed as a bedsheet flopped onto its face
And three or four dragging fenceposts barked its rear ankles and shins.

It tripped and fell breaking through the fence again on the far
Side of the field, but struggled up once more to crash
Into the undergrowth and disappear amid the trees.

Lastly, like stunned townspeople in the wake of a twister,
My neighbor and I picked up the strewn pieces of clothing
As we followed tracks, like post-holes, into the dented woods.

Blackberry War

I do not often go looking for black.
Afraid of the old dark all my life, I've learned
To be in darkness and control my fear,
Learned how rare it is to find true darkness.
It's found deep in new moon woods on starless nights
Or in the windowless cellar of a house
With the door shut tight at the top of the steps
And the metal bulkhead padlocked outside.
War is another way into the black:
The tracers and coffins I need not recount.

Instead, I will take my white, plastic quart
Containers up the dust trails to Mutton Hill
And gently pick the oversized berries,
Black as the darkest thoughts of man but sweet
As darkness never becomes. There on the hill,
At the hot end of August, when most plants are leaning
Toward ruin, and there's neither a house nor a light,
I will pick black thoughts, one thought per berry,
And taste a few as well, and wonder what's new
With the war; when it's late, and the world leans toward ruin.

October Elegy

It's the sixth. Today snow flurries fell twice.
Three days ago the leaves peaked; now the peaks
Are frosted white. Robins puff with winter plumage.
My breath appears like a ghost of summer.

Two friends, two losses: one lost a father,
The other a daughter. I sit staring
Into fire, wondering when I'll be seasoned
Enough to burn. Whose eyes will my smoke water?

Today wet leaves covered the tractor tires:
Red, orange, yellow. And for once the geese
Actually flew due south. I look for truth
In the mundane facts of life, facts of death.

I counted forty-four geese and I heard them.
One snowflake caught on my lash and blurred.

Going Under The Barn

— after Adrienne Rich

First, having been told
by my neighbor, "It's best
to let your barn breathe,"
I pried with the hammer's claw
the plywood skirt
connecting my barn to the ground.

It smelled like opening a grave.

Cardboard boxes, emptied of their poison
littered the shadows
and the corpse of a squirrel.

It was a carpenter's dump:
two by fours, slats, plywood, old steps,
all with nails sticking out,
bent nails, rusty nails, some easily snapped off.

There was scrap metal:
an old stovepipe,
tins for meat, crackers, and cocoa,
a heavy steel rod
ten feet long
for God knows what.

One hundred years of past owners
dealt with things thus,
stuffing them under the barn:

an antique laundry wringer,
a dead tractor battery,
a rabbit hutch.

From outside, I saw all this
and more, as the barn breathed.
For weeks, I put off my chore.

The flashlight beam led me in.

I crawled under boards
the horses had rattled
bringing in the hay.

On my back, I wriggled
under planks not quite flush
so dust, dirt, and mouse droppings
had fallen through cracks
and piled up in a shallow sift.

I followed the path
other men had made, crawling
through the waste and rubble:

hunks of macadam
from the fractured driveway,
chunks of foundation stone.

The path led to pipes
and wires, and a dryer vent hose,
for the barn is connected to the house.

I crawled under the barn
to replace the dryer vent hose
and found spiders
that live without sun
and a chipmunk nest.
I heard mice scurrying.

Men had come and gone there
cussing as I cussed,
bleeding as I bled,
leaving a tape measure
or claw hammer behind
by mistake
to find months later
when going under the barn again
could not be put off any longer.

There were no monsters,
just the closeness of the den,
the darkness of the cave climbed out of
at the dawn of man.

I remembered that Stone Age
while under the barn
and remembered my own dawn
with its devils in the night.

I kept my head low,
but it's hard to gauge,
in the mostly pitch black,
what's beam, what's air.

I cut myself and sweated,
so that crawling out, head first,
with a caul of cobwebs, dead bugs and grime
clinging to me, I was a sight.

And the common light of day
Was a new light.

Finale

Carving Your Future

My mother said I'd never make it selling knives
though she said once I ought to be a dictator
of a third world country.
                          Well I found that country.
I found my people and I waved my sword: a knife,
double-edged and fork-tipped, complete with fish-scaler,
and the first thing I told them, speaking through a mike
clipped to my shirt collar, was that I don't sell knives.
I sell pardons, and relics, and talismans. I sell hope,
belief, faith, and self-esteem. I save marriages
and battered kids. I sell knives out of a wooden
booth I've pulled behind my pickup from Fryeburg, Maine
to West Point, Mississippi. I work agricultural
and harvest fairs in most counties--my knives
and all those blue ribbon pies--and I've spread the word
inside and out of Sears, K-mart, Wal-Mart and some
Jordan Marsh stores.
                     I hold up a knife and say,
"Friends, any number of kitchen utensils will do
the food miracles I am about to perform.
I know most of you have carrot peelers,
onion-slicers, apple-corers, melon-ballers, and enough
culinary accoutrements to arm a small
yet lethal S.W.A.T. team. If you don't mind opening
a drawer and pulling out half a dozen or so
steel, wooden, and plastic preparatory tools
and if you don't mind spending the extra seconds
putting one down and picking up another--hell,
who would mind?--then you might, and I stress the word, might,
you might not need this knife of highest quality
stainless steel finished in Switzerland and shipped here
in bulk so I can sell it for twenty dollars
minus one penny plus tax and still pay my bills
with a small profit. I sleep well each night
dreaming of my happy customers making palm trees
from carrots and green peppers, or, less aesthetic-minded,
but more pleasing to the palate, the dream
of a fine lady I met in Goshen, Vermont,
a Mrs. Lucia Babcock, who makes a fine five-bean salad.

I never forget a customer. And I've sold
15,000 of these hand-honed, flame-tempered,
one-sixteenth of an inch thick PVC plastic super-
strong-handled, mini-machete-mighted,
filet-knife-graced, all purpose, never failing kitchen knives.

I'm an honest man, friends, and it wouldn't be right
to not tell you that seven of my knives have failed;
more specifically, the handles failed. I replaced
all seven. Still, you might, and I stress the word, might,
you might not need this knife. Not if you go to bed
with a smile on your face each night. Not if you look
at friends and foes alike: straight in the eye.
Not if the young and the old both love and trust you, and grace
is a condiment you seldom reach for in life
so well cured and evenly simmered are your days.
No, you upright, respectable, hardworking folks,
you might not need this knife that can chop coconuts
in half and hull strawberries and open raw clams
and oysters and whittle oak and pry off fan belts,
hubcaps and flat tires from wheel rims and fly true
as a brass-tipped, feather-tailed dart and skin
seals, bears, and rattlesnakes and perform C-sections
and tracheotomies (instructions are engraved
in the blade to assist with these emergency
procedures). Yes, my friends, you might not feel a tinge
of guilt for turning down such an affordable
life-saving device. But as I said, folks, I'm not
here just to sell you knives.
                              We've all got too many knives
already, don't we? But this isn't just a knife.
Excalibur wasn't just a sword. Jim Bowie
didn't wield just any old knife. **Aztecs
didn't cut pulsing hearts out with butter
knives!** (pardon me folks, I'm getting excited).
Surgeons need more than God to save babies;
they need knives, scalpels, miracle workers.
And this here is a miracle knife.

Trust in the stainless steel, the sharp edge, the sure grip.
Isn't it attractive? Doesn't it gleam
with all you have yet to do? . . . Radishes
trimmed expertly, a watermelon carved
into a green striped billboard for the church picnic:
'He Is Risen!' . . . A chain-link fence, sawed through,
wire by wire, as you escape from an oppressive,
most likely communist institution. You're with me,
my friends, if you've ever been inspired
just by looking at a photo or picture
of a loved one. You're with me if the sun
rising each day is an invitation.
You're with me if you think each American
should stress the two words spelled by the last four letters
of the word, 'American': ' . . . I can.'

Now, my friends, take a few seconds
after the show; I'll demonstrate for you,
one-on-one. I'll show you how to remove
wine corks, filet a northern pike, spackle
a ceiling, pick locks, cut diamonds,
and notch a lodgepole pine. That's $19.99."

Douglas "Woody" Woodsum has taught at two universities and five public schools. He has published poetry, prose, and cartoons in many magazines, newspapers, and anthologies, including *Yankee, Maine Times, The Café Review, Prairie Schooner, Antioch Review, English Journal, Off The Coast, Southern Review, Denver Quarterly, Exquisite Corpse, Massachusetts Review, Michigan Quarterly Review, Puckerbrush Review, Down East, The Iowa Review, New England Review* and *The Beloit Poetry Journal.* His work has been broadcast on Maine Public Radio. He is a former Ruth Lilly poet, a two-time Avery Hopwood Award winner, a *Maine Times* fiction prizewinner, and a winner of the Bread Loaf Poetry Prize. His work is online at Poetry Daily and www.fishousepoems.org. In 1995, he changed his focus from his own writing to teach high school English in rural Maine. God help him. With his students, he has published ten annual anthologies of oral history and folklore. Raised on the Maine coast, he now lives with the artist Donna Asmussen in Smithfield, Maine.